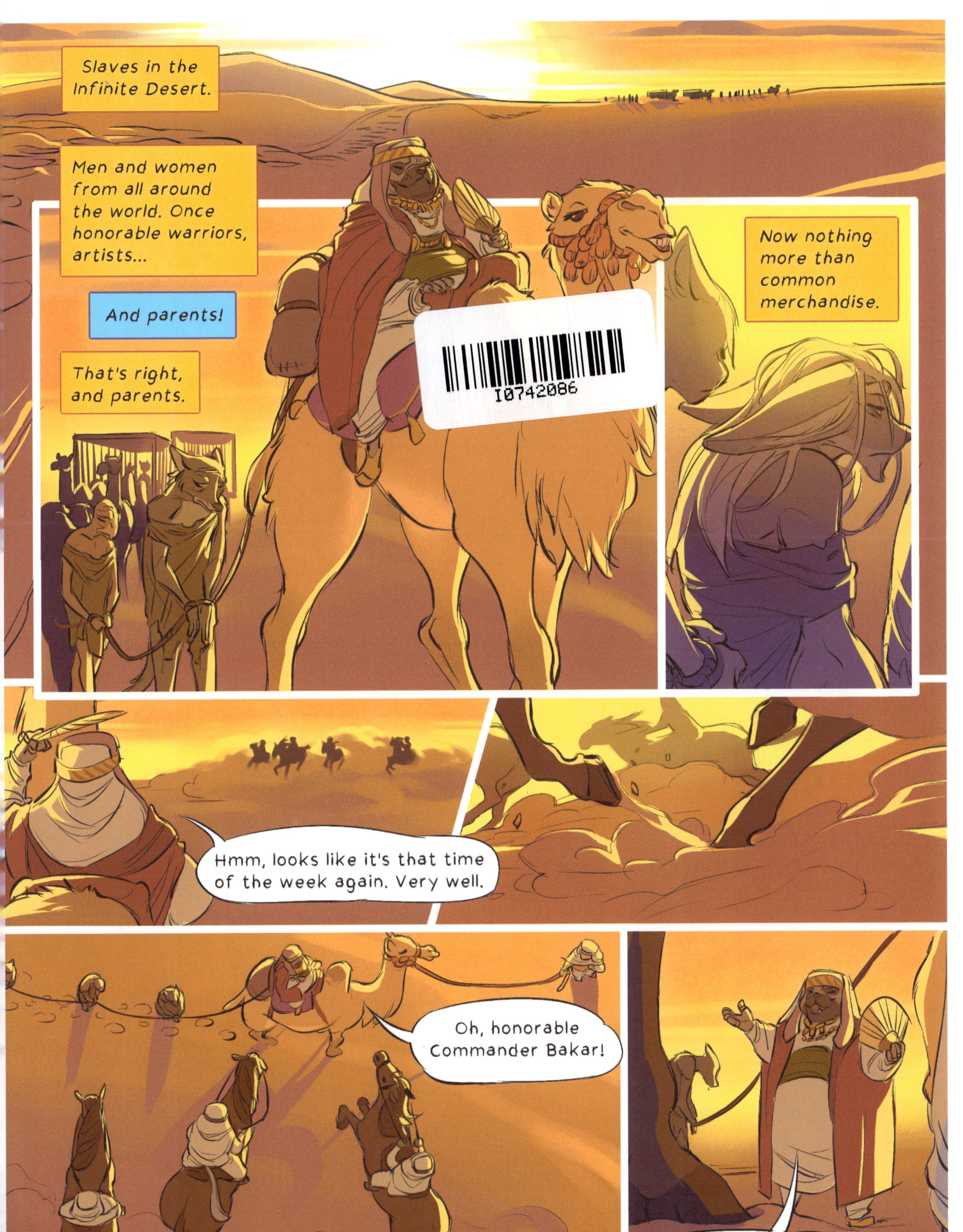
Slaves in the Infinite Desert.
Men and women from all around the world. Once honorable warriors, artists...
And parents!
That's right, and parents.
Now nothing more than common merchandise.
Hmm, looks like it's that time of the week again. Very well.
Oh, honorable Commander Bakar!
How can I be of your service this time?

We want to see the slaves, Nizaar.
And unclothe all of them, like always.
As you wish my lord.
CLAP CLAP CLAP
Merchandise, which did not count as living, sentient creatures any more.
None of them are the one. Show me the rest!

My lord, I already told you, if you would tell me in advance what kind of slave you would be interested in, it would be much easier to obtain if we know what to look for.
As you wish.
It's not your business! Just show me the rest!
Slaves have no present, nor future. They live, then they die like they never existed.
That is a bit too dark...
Where was I?
Oh yes. But this is not the end that awaits for all of them.
?
I know, that's the point. It will only get better from this point.
Oh, indeed!

Because for one of them...
The Key...
WE FOUND THE KEY!
BAFF
...the gods ordained another kind of destiny.
But it's true.
That is such a cliche...
Please, let me continue.
Oh, right. Sorry.
Still...

And for this one slave, named Shen...
Hihi!
Stop smiling...
NO!
Anyway...
For this one slave, the path assigned by the gods completely changed his life.
5

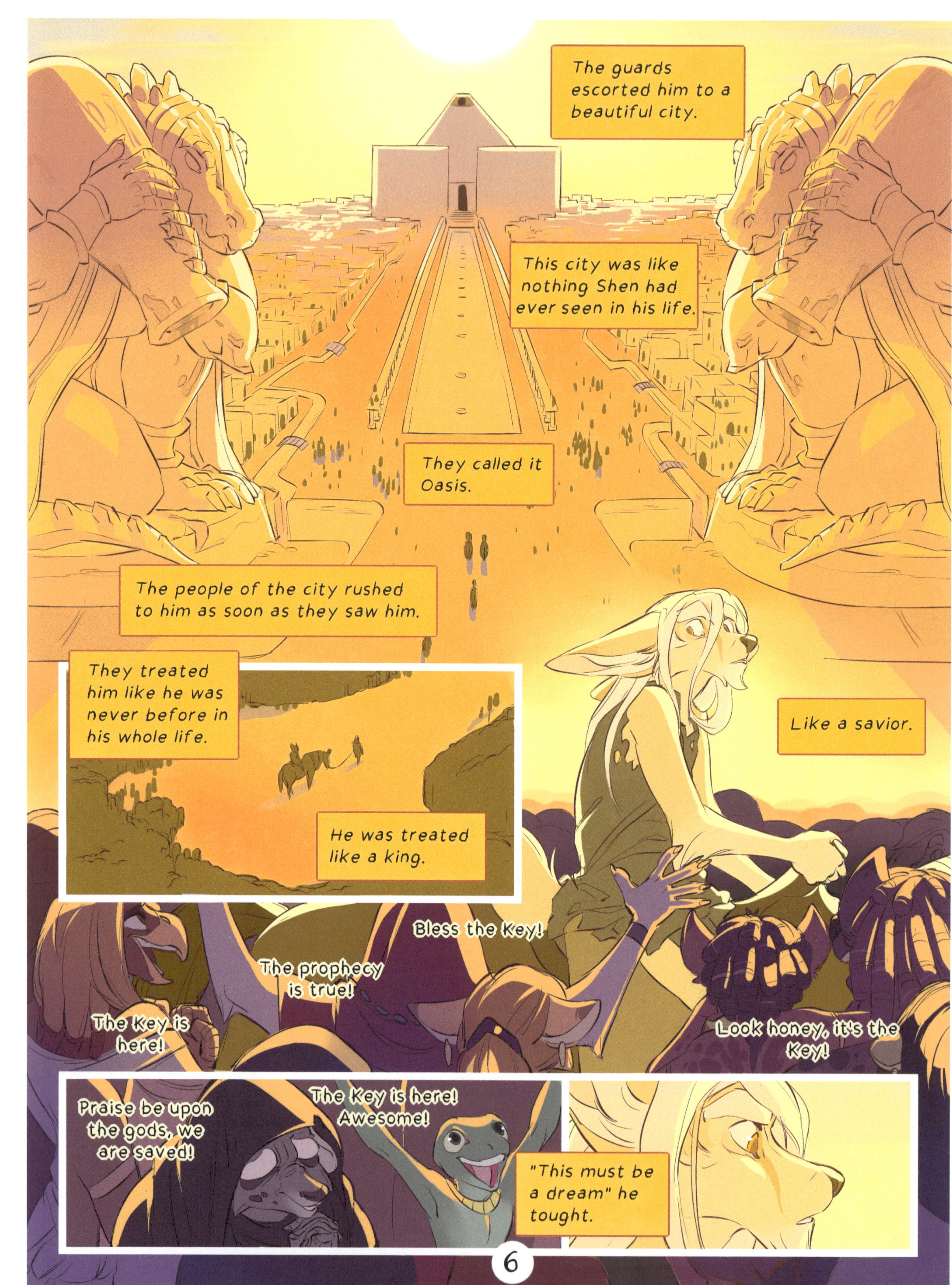

The guards escorted him to a beautiful city.
This city was like nothing Shen had ever seen in his life.
They called it Oasis.
The people of the city rushed to him as soon as they saw him.
They treated him like he was never before in his whole life.
He was treated like a king.
Like a savior.
Bless the Key!
The prophecy is true!
The Key is here!
Look honey, it's the Key!
Praise be upon the gods, we are saved!
The Key is here! Awesome!
"This must be a dream" he tought.

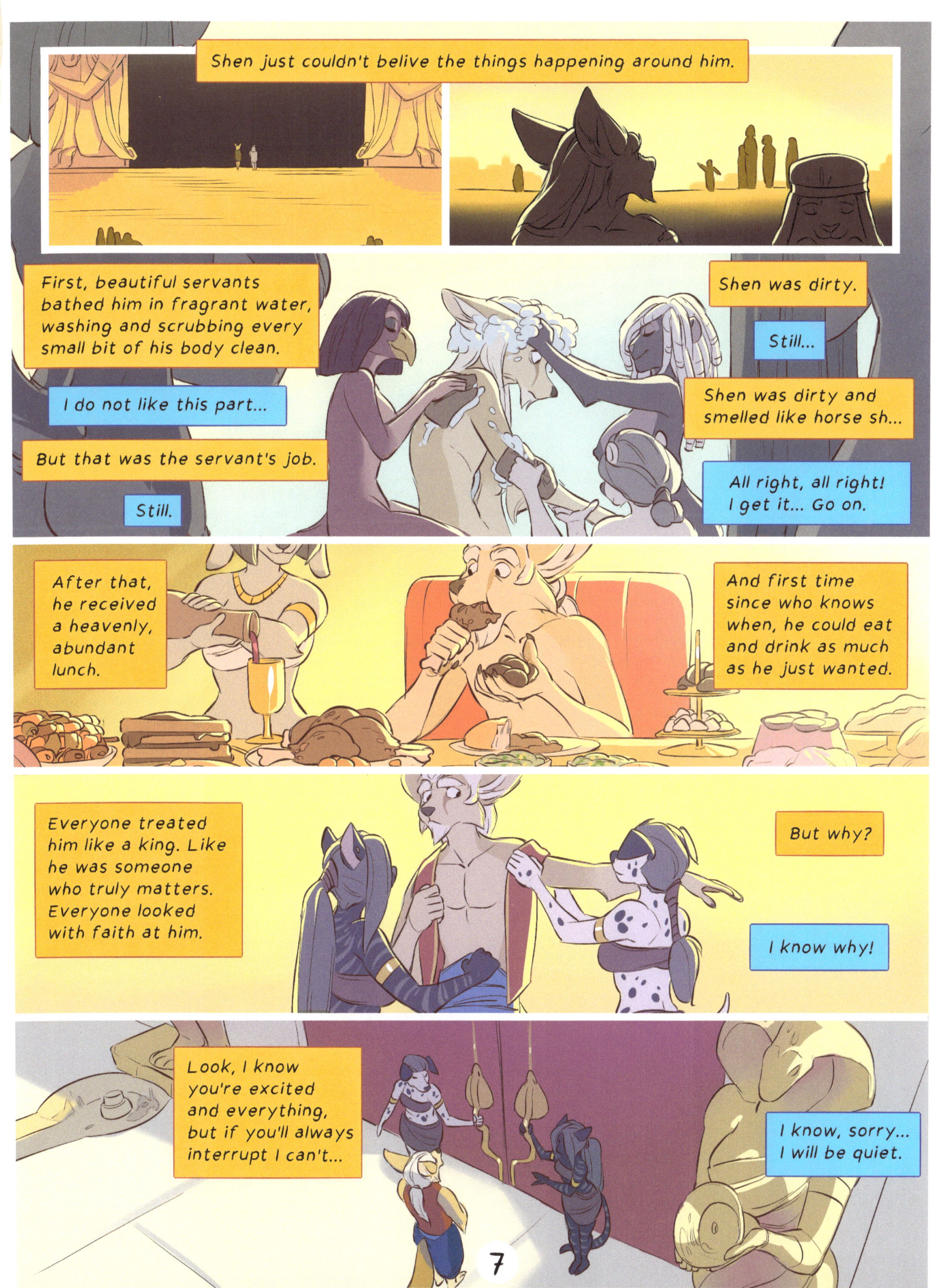

Shen just couldn't belive the things happening around him.
First, beautiful servants bathed him in fragrant water, washing and scrubbing every small bit of his body clean.
I do not like this part...
But that was the servant's job.
Still.
Shen was dirty.
Still...
Shen was dirty and smelled like horse sh...
All right, all right! I get it... Go on.
After that, he received a heavenly, abundant lunch.
And first time since who knows when, he could eat and drink as much as he just wanted.
Everyone treated him like a king. Like he was someone who truly matters. Everyone looked with faith at him.
But why?
I know why!
Look, I know you're excited and everything, but if you'll always interrupt I can't...
I know, sorry... I will be quiet.

SPLOSH
He is finally here!
HE HAS ARRIVED!
Thank you girls, please, leave us alone now!
I am so happy you are here!
Well...
Me too...
I mean...
8

Greetings! I am Zaphira, ruler of the Infinite Desert, and Queen of Oasis. What is your name?
I'm Shen... It's a pleasure to meet you, your highness...
My pleasure Shen! But you can call me Zaphira.
The first time Shen laid his eyes on the queen, he became petrified.
Those eyes were the kindest, most honest, and most gorgeous ones Shen had ever seen in his life.
Is... that true?
Yes, that was exactly what he saw in them. Honesty, and kindness.
That sounds beautiful...
Would you be so kind to take off your clothes?
I... If you wish... But... I mean...
Oh, do not be afraid dear Shen. There is absolutely nothing to be worried about.
Well... If you insist, your highness...
IT IS YOU INDEED!
The one my people were waiting for such a long time!
This is just a simple birthmark my queen. I have it since the day I was born.
And I'm no one... Just a simple slave...

Do not be silly Shen, you are the Key! You are a slave no more.
I had a feeling like that, yeah...
You know, there is an ancient prophecy, written in a long forgotten language.
Although we are unable to translate the whole text, what we could understand states that in the time of great need, the Key will come to our aid in the guise of a common slave, and by opening the sacred Lock, it will bring redemption to the people of Oasis and the Infinite Desert.
But what's the key... And what's the lock, your highness?
Please, just call me Zaphira.
And not what, but who. YOU are the Key Shen. You are the key to the future of my people.
A Lock, a Key, a prophecy, and in the focus of all of this stands Shen, who was just a common slave this morning.
And at that moment, he got petrified again!
Oh, he did indeed!
And I am the sacred Lock, chosen by the gods themselves. That is why I was born. That is the whole purpose of my existence.
10

Come Shen!
Let us not waste more time!
What...?
PUSH
Even if Shen was petrified...
But he was not petrified ENOUGH!
Right?
Well...
Riiiight? Hihi!
You know what? Right. Can't hurt a bit of irony.
But for Shen's luck, Queen Zaphira saw the need for her help.
Oh, I see there will be need for my help.
And she was prepared for this possibility as well.
Yes, I am prepared for this possibility as well.
And she knew EXACTLY what to do.
I know EXACTLY what to do.
I think you'll still need a bit more practice in this.
I know, I know...
Hm, how was it? Let see...
Yes. Chapter 2, section 12.

You... I mean... Me...
And after that...
Yes.
Section 16, I believe.
Then section 22...
And for the last part...
Yes, section 25.
MMMM...
I am almost finished. This is so exciting, is it not?
SUCK SUCK SUCK
Oh look!
LOOK!
It worked! We can finally begin!
You would not believe how long I have been waiting for this sacred day.
You... did?
Yes! I am so happy that we found you at last. I have been dreaming about this moment for my whole life.

And with my training, it will only take a few minutes.
What training...?
You know, I practiced a lot.
I will not even need to use my hands.
I was really looking forward to this day, and I did not want to make any mistakes...
...so I just memorised the whole chapter.
What do you think?
Am I doing good?
SMACK
More than... good...
It is such a relief to hear that! So all those nights spent studying were worth it!

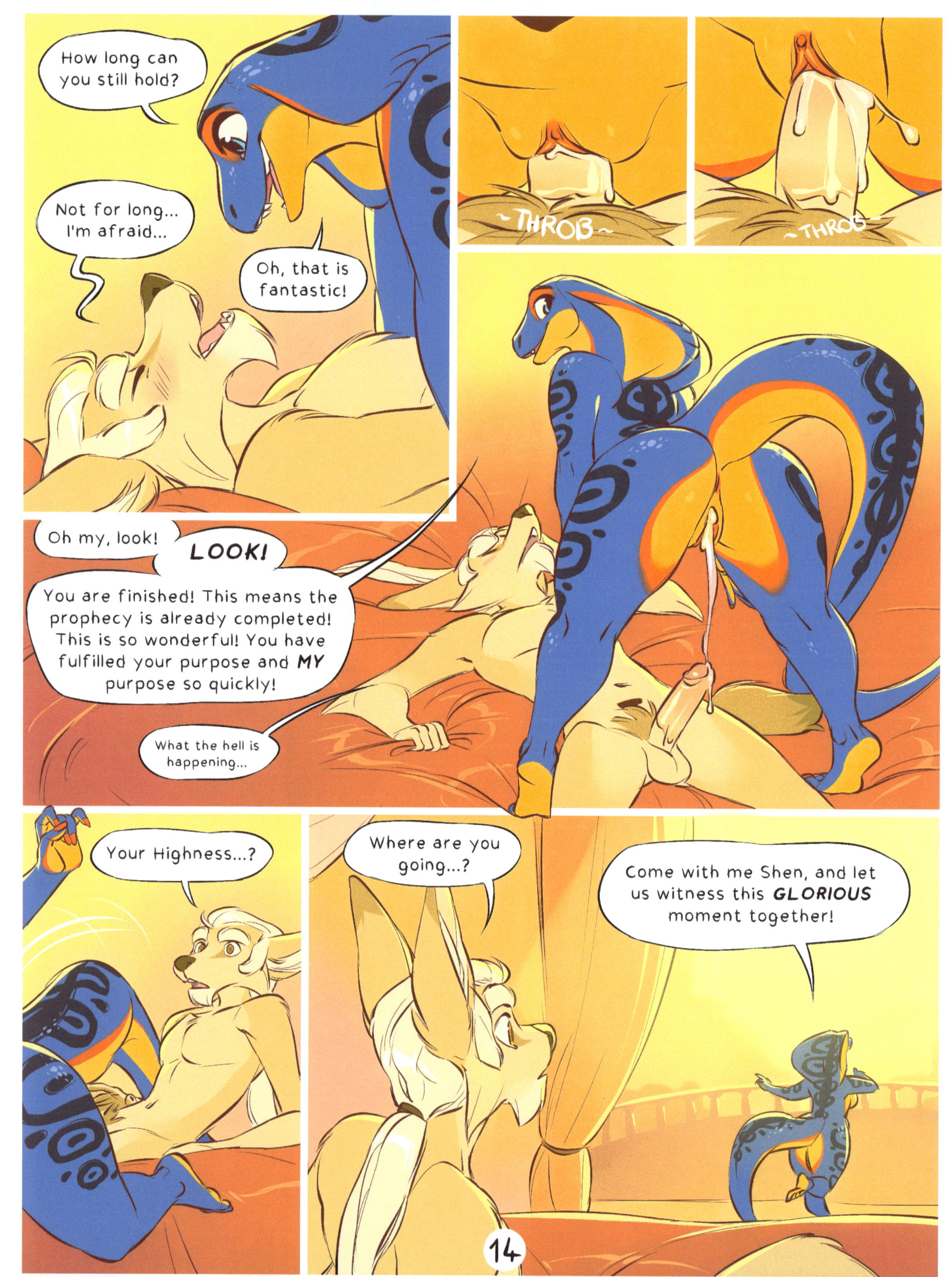

How long can you still hold?
Not for long... I'm afraid...
Oh, that is fantastic!
~THROB~
~THROB~
Oh my, look!
LOOK!
You are finished! This means the prophecy is already completed! This is so wonderful! You have fulfilled your purpose and MY purpose so quickly!
What the hell is happening...
Your Highness...?
Where are you going...?
Come with me Shen, and let us witness this GLORIOUS moment together!
14

COME SHEN! QUICKLY!
Belive me, this holy moment you do not...
...want...
...to...
...miss...?
What...?
Why is nothing happening?
Is there something wrong?
What do you mean by "taught"?
I did everything as I was taught by the priestesses.
What could I possibly do wrong?
And I learned ALL the lessons, there is no way I missed anything!
Nothing...?
Your highness? Why did you run away?
My queen? Are you even listening to me...?
I do not understand...
Wait, I got it!
I BELIEVE I KNOW WHAT WAS THE PROBLEM!
It is SO obvious! Such tiny detail, no wonder even the priestesses overlooked it.
What... tiny detail...?

It is not the lock that goes into the key, but the OTHER WAY AROUND! The key is the one going into the lock!
But your highness, I don't...
Come now Shen, place your key into my lock, and open the gate to a brighter future!
Just call me Zaphira, I told you.
And as I said, I am not your ruler, and you are not one of my subjects.
You are my destiny.
Do not worry. All will be well. Fate ordained you for this task, just like it did me. This is our fate.
Our purpose.
You... saved me, and made me a free man once again. I'd do what ever you just wish. But I don't know if I'm worthy enough to...
And Shen, in the queen's calm smile saw that she was certain. And at that moment, he truly knew, he truly felt that at the end, all will be well.
Did he? Truly?
Yes, he did.
And so, without him even knowing...
...he took the next step to fulfill his destiny.
Alright then, I do as you wish.
16

AAAH♥
Mmm♥
¡AAAAAAAH!♥
Oh no! I'm so sorry! Did it hurt?
Oh, not at all! Quite the opposite...
I did not know this could be... such a pleasant feeling. But after all, I am not used to do it like this.
Like this? You mean... you've never been on bottom before?
No, why would I? Anyway, I'm just a little embarrassed by my unexpected reaction, that is all...
But please continue, and promise me not to hold back when you are close to finishing, okay?
Alright. Then... I won't hold it back...

I do not understand what has gotten into me...
Mmm...
Aahn...
Mmmmm♥
Oooh...
Oodoh...
Oooh♥ This feels so...
...boundlessly calming and delightful...
I'm very happy to hear that, but...
SQUEEEZE

I'm sorry, but I just can't hold it back any longer!
Do not hold it back Shen!
Let it all out, and make our prophecy come true!
Ahhh...
I have NEVER felt anything like this in my entire life.
I can safely say the same...
Good job there Shen.
Good job.
Hm?
I felt such an unfamiliar, yet overwhelming pleasure, it MUST have been a sign from the gods! The prophecy MUST have came true!
Come Shen!
Let us FINALLY witness the coming of the prophecy together!
-sigh-
Your Highness, I believe...
PAT PAT

But...
Why is nothing happening...?
Why?
What is missing?
...am I doing wrong...?
What...
Your highness. You still haven't told me...
What could it be?
What?
Your highness...?
But...
The Key and the Lock DID connect.
Did they not...?
Yes...
I believe they did.
Wait!
Wait...
By the gods!
I... I believe I know what the REAL problem was!
I know what to do!
Quickly Shen!
Wh... what?
I know Shen, I KNOW!

I am such a fool!
I should have been wiser as the leader of Oasis.
The Key and the Lock are not just simple tools.
They aren't?
No, they are not.
WE are the Key and the Lock, so our bodies AND our souls have to become one as well.
As precisely a key and a lock fits together, our souls shall fit as such.
Come Shen!
Let us connect our souls!
Would you... excuse me for a moment...?
Gkk..

You just stay right there, I will be back in a moment.
Alright, if you say so...

Wha...?

Wow...
A secret door?

And there she goes again.
I wonder if she'll explain anything at the end.

This whole situation is starting to get really bizarre.
All this prophecy and birthmark mess is just...

BAM
THUD
THUD
THUD
Huh?

THUD
THUD
Maybe I should...
NOOO!
No, I really shouldn't mess around in a queen's...
Your highness?

Your highness?
Are you okay?
THUD
THUD
BAM
AAAGGHHH!!!
Damnit! Where the hell is that switch?

Damn it!
TAP
TAP
WHERE IS IT?
TAP
TAP
CLICK
YES!
Found it!
WOW!
What is this place?
This... This looks like a hidden library!
But how? This room is too tall to fit in the top of the palace.
Could it be...?
Could it be a magical room?
There must be THOUSANDS of books here!
Unbelievable! I can't even see the top of it! It's like it goes on forever!
What... are you doing here my Queen?
I heard you screaming. What happened?
Your Highness?
LIL POKE
AAAA
AAAHH

YOU scared me!
YOU scared me!
How did YOU get in here?
YOU walked through the secret door right in front of me!
Oh no! I really did that...
These books...
Are these about the prophecy?
Wait...
But this is...
This is just an ordinary romantic novel!
Let's see the rest...
This one is about pirates. Another romantic novel, but with angels and demons.
This one is about dragons and dungeons.
This has nothing to do with the prophecy. This is... my personal... secret library...
Wait a minute...
Are ALL of these books adventure and romantic novels?
What kind of library is this? And what does it have to do with the prophecy?
Passion of the sea
Gift from the Water God
Eternal Love
Eternal
The Snow Heavens
24

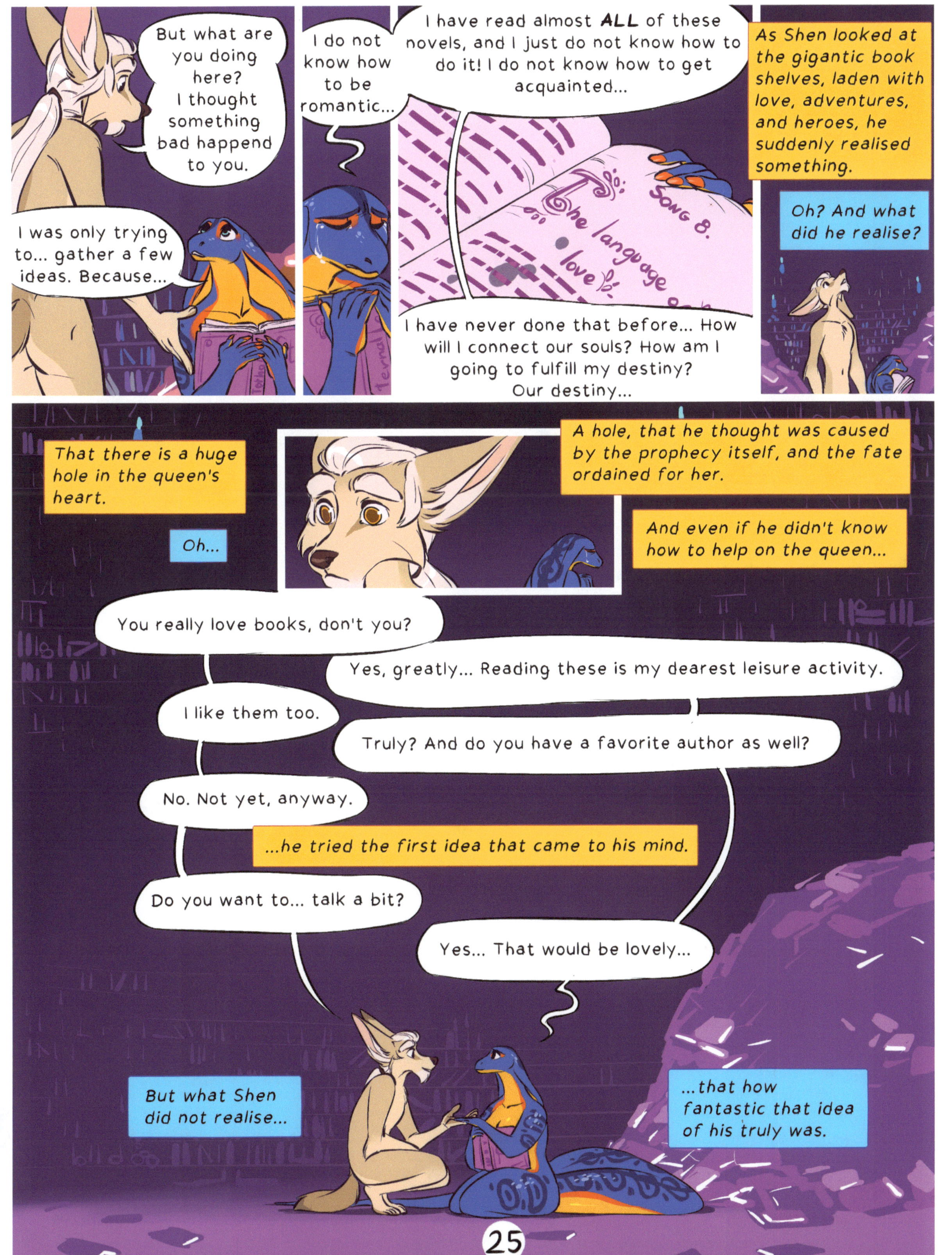

But what are you doing here? I thought something bad happend to you.
I was only trying to... gather a few ideas. Because...
I do not know how to be romantic...
I have read almost ALL of these novels, and I just do not know how to do it! I do not know how to get acquainted...
I have never done that before... How will I connect our souls? How am I going to fulfill my destiny? Our destiny...
As Shen looked at the gigantic book shelves, laden with love, adventures, and heroes, he suddenly realised something.
Oh? And what did he realise?
That there is a huge hole in the queen's heart.
Oh...
A hole, that he thought was caused by the prophecy itself, and the fate ordained for her.
And even if he didn't know how to help on the queen...
You really love books, don't you?
Yes, greatly... Reading these is my dearest leisure activity.
I like them too.
Truly? And do you have a favorite author as well?
No. Not yet, anyway.
...he tried the first idea that came to his mind.
Do you want to... talk a bit?
Yes... That would be lovely...
But what Shen did not realise...
...that how fantastic that idea of his truly was.

The language of love
Song 8.

I would never imagine that you adore reading as well!
I think that's a bit of an overstatement, but I like novels in general. Aaand my parents beat me quite a few times for spending my time reading instead of working...
This is fantastic!
It wasn't too pleasant, believe me.
No, I mean we are talking right now.
I am most certain this is exactly what we have to do to connect our souls.
I see this prophecy is really important to you.
This is the only reason of my existence.
I'm sorry, but that sounds awfully sad...
Not at all, the prophecy is a fantastic thing!
But what would you like to chat about?
We could start by you telling me like, anything about this prophecy of yours, and...
Absolutely not! We should work on getting to know each other, and stop wasting time on obvious things.
About myself? That will be an easy one. I am the ruler of Oasis, the chosen one born with the mark of the prophecy , who are going to fulfill the ancient and holy prophecy.
Yes, you talked about that a few times already. But who are you beside all that?
So, what topic would you like to discuss?
Alright... Then tell me a bit more about yourself.

Me? Well... I am... I think... So... I am the ruler of Oasis, the chosen one, who...
I got that, really. But what are you going to do AFTER you... I mean, we, fulfilled the prophecy?
After... that... I will...
You know what, it doesn't matter. Just forget it. Let me ask you something else. Who is Zaphira, as a person? Not the Queen of Oasis, but Zaphira, who sits in front of me. Who is she?
You know what, let's just try it from a different angle. What do you do, when you are NOT busy managing your empire?
Umm... I... She is...
She is the ruler of Oasis, the chosen one born with the mark of the prophecy, who...
That is easy! I love reading all kinds of novels!
Great! And what else do you like to do? Do you have any other hobby?
Well... Well...
I am sorry, but I just can not do this...
I do not know how to... How to do this...
At that moment, looking at the annihilating desperation on the queen's face, Shen had a feeling that this prophecy demanded more from the queen than just some love making studies.
27

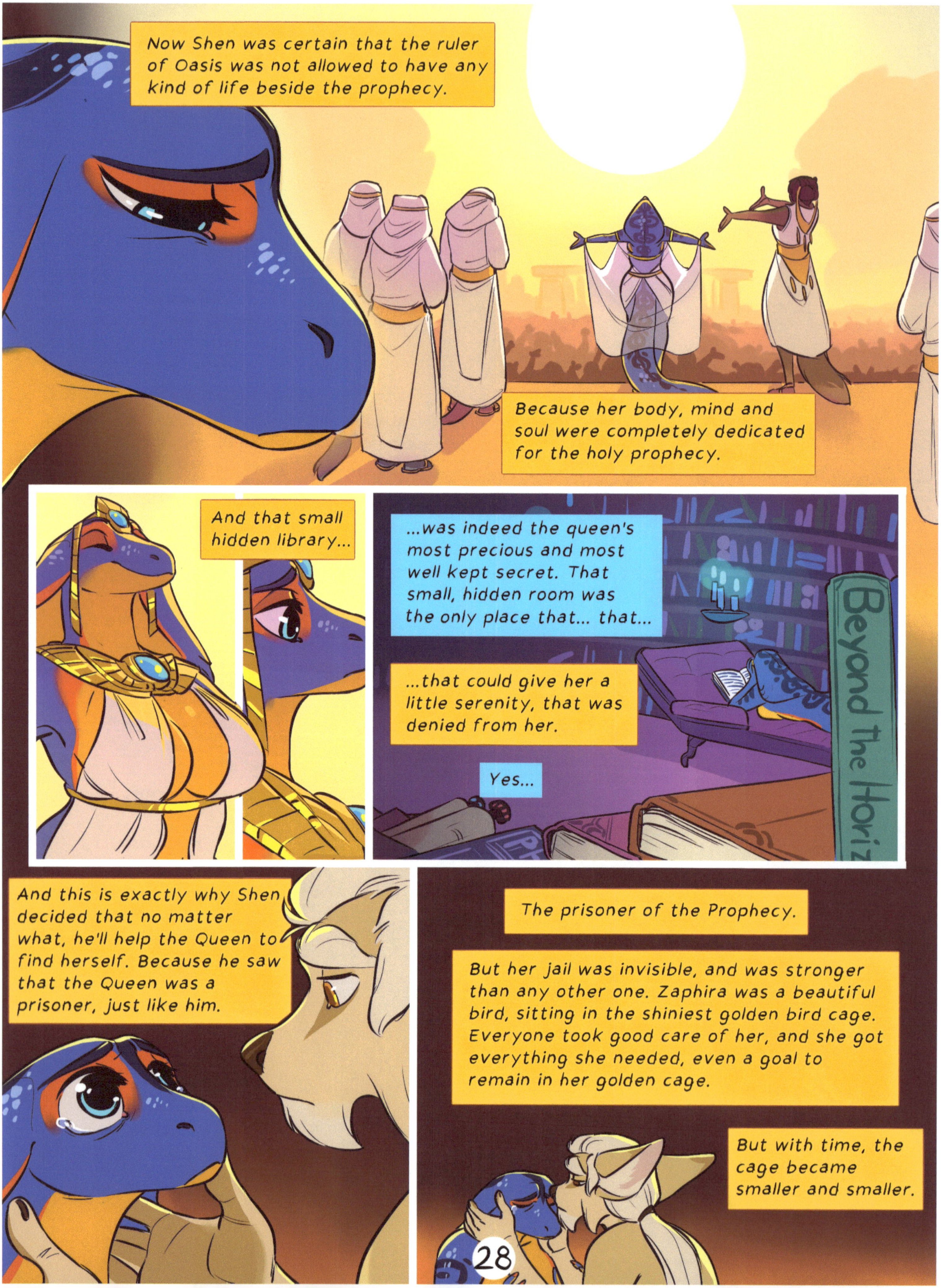

Now Shen was certain that the ruler of Oasis was not allowed to have any kind of life beside the prophecy.

Because her body, mind and soul were completely dedicated for the holy prophecy.

And that small hidden library...

...was indeed the queen's most precious and most well kept secret. That small, hidden room was the only place that... that...

...that could give her a little serenity, that was denied from her.

Yes...

Beyond the Horiz

And this is exactly why Shen decided that no matter what, he'll help the Queen to find herself. Because he saw that the Queen was a prisoner, just like him.

The prisoner of the Prophecy.

But her jail was invisible, and was stronger than any other one. Zaphira was a beautiful bird, sitting in the shiniest golden bird cage. Everyone took good care of her, and she got everything she needed, even a goal to remain in her golden cage.

But with time, the cage became smaller and smaller.

I have an idea!
What do you say if we'd "play" a romantic story?
What do you mean by that?
I'm sure you have your favorite scenes from those novels too. Let's play that we are in one of those. What is that could NEVER be absent from a great romantic story?
Hmm...
Yes, a dinner! An intimate candlelight dinner!
Exactly!
BOOP
Maybe... I think...
CLAP CLAP CLAP
Wow, that was unreasonably fast!
I know this is not much, but I hope it will be enough for a proper romantic dinner.
29

...and sometimes I have even read them through the whole night, without sleeping a single minute!

I would have actually bet on that. I assume you have read all of them.

I have indeed! A few of them even multiple times already.

And what grabs you in novels and books?

Because I saw all kinds of books there, like romantic, adventure, horror. I mean, if there wouldn't be anything generally interesting in them, you wouldn't love and collect them with such enthusiasm.

Well... I believe... Perhaps...

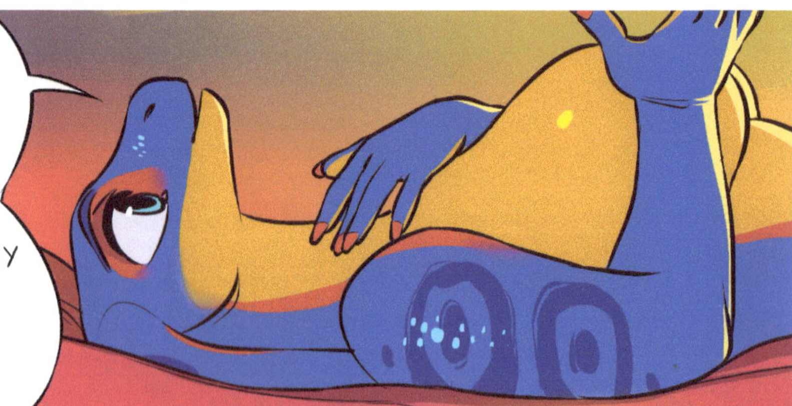

Opening a book is like opening a door to a completely different world. A good novel can put you in the character's skin, so it becomes YOU who explores unfamiliar and fantastic places, solve mysteries, and defeat evil.

And the romantic novels... Ah, those are my favorites! I just adore the idea of two people who love each other from the bottom of their heart, longing to spend their whole life with each other...

That must be...

...such a pleasant thing.

Hmm. You know, you mentioned something I just can't get over.

And what would it be?

Yes, that is correct.
I have been born with the mark of the prophecy. That is the main reason I have become the queen and religious leader of Oasis. And as a leader I had to be prepared to meet the Key.
I had to practice a lot to satisfy their high expectations.
I was trained my whole life by the priestesses to be able to fulfill my task as fast and efficient as possible.
You said you've never been on bottom, and... That you were trained for the whole act?
So you've never done it because you... wanted to?
Why... why would I ever do that? My purpose is to fulfill the prophecy, by...
I know... I know...
Erm... you know, in my favorite romantic stories, the lovebirds always feed each other in a very passionate way. Maybe we could try that out too.
That sounds WONDERFUL!
Please, close your eyes, I would like to be the one to start!
As you wish.
AHHGRIII
Oh no, this is not the way to do it, am I right?
No - GHKKK - I don't think so...

Forgive me, I am just... so nervous right now...
Don't worry, it's okay...
Then please allow me to show it.
The sweetest bite...
...for the sweetest lady.
Awww!
This is truly the most romantic thing I have ever experienced.
Me next!
Just gently.
Like this?
Exactly like this.
Shen... I'm so ashamed, you had no chance to talk about yourself so far, or... I just simply did not give you any chance to speak... Please, would you be so kind to tell me more about yourself? Naturally, only if it does not make you feel uncomfortable.
I'm sorry my queen...
Zaphira.
...but I'm afraid I have to disappoint you.
There's really not much to tell about myself. I was born, and lived with my family through out my whole life in a tiny village, far from here to the west.
My life was as boring and as monotonous as it gets.
But two years ago a barbarian tribe raided our village. Anyone that wasn't killed was sold as a slave. I became a slave, my family... didn't.
Since then they passed me from hand to hand as a disposable tool, and...

Now I'm here, only thanks to you.
I see... I mean...
And this time it was Zaphira's turn to guide the discourse into a better direction.
I'm sorry...
Don't worry, it's okay.
What would you say...
...if I would give you the next bite like this?
You... like it?
You have no idea.
Was it... really that enjoyable...?
Truly the most enjoyable bite I ever had.
Then please...
...have another.

Oh my! This one looks even tastier!
Tehehe! That tickles!
But do not stop please!
But only if...
I mean...
Are you embarrassed? Even though we recently made love like... twice already?
Yes but... that was only my duty. This here is... different... I have never felt anything like this before. This could be similar to what... those characters in those novels could feel. I am...
I am truly enjoying spending this whole day with you, Shen.
Then I might know something else that should NEVER be missing from any good romantic novel.
And what would it be?

Dance.
Oh, indeed! How could I forget? That truly should not be missing!
You truly have such a VAST knowledge about romantic situations!
Hehe, no need to exaggerate my sweet queen. I'm sure I haven't read NEARLY as many romantic novels as you.
Still, it seems you somehow understand their formula a lot better.
Haha, it has nothing to do with science.
Then I shall call for the musicians immediately.
There's no need for them.

Dancing without music?
People said I'm tone-deaf anyway. And a fumbler.
Let's just do it like this.
Just the two of us.
That sounds truly wonderful.
I have never in my life danced like this.
Without music?
No. Like this.
This is so endlessly pleasant...

You have such gorgeous eyes my queen.
They are stunning.
Oh... really? Thank you. That is so nice of you.
They are so blue. I've only witnessed such shimmering beauty at the sea.
You... you have seen the sea?
Nobody ever told you how beautiful they are?
No... Never...
But they truly are! I've never seen such beautiful and kind eyes before.
Really?
Yes.
And I'd love to dive deep into your sea, and get to know all of it's beauty, mystery, and...
...pain.
There is one thing I... Well... You know... I wanted to ask from you.
I'm all ears.
When you asked me how I would describe myself... I could not give you an answer.
But you... So... How do you see... me?
37

Never in my life have I seen a more beautiful thing like you.
But that doesn't really matter.
It does not?
No. Because never in my life have I seen a kinder, sweeter, angel than you.
Oh, well... Oh! That was... That was very sweet of you. You left me completely speechless...
And... This might be a rather strange question, but I can not get it out of my mind. Do you not see... anything weird on me?
Weird? What do you mean by that?
Like... I do not know... I am tied to my duty so tight that I feel my behavior and look just...
Shhh.
Stop right there. You are perfect as you are. Believe me.
But I think there was something that surprised me at first.
And what was that?
You promise you won't take it amiss?
I will not! I swear!
I've never met your kind before. I've only seen scaled folks from afar. Their skin always looked so cold and damp to me. Then you came, you touched me, you nestled to me and...
And your skin was so incredibly soft and warm. It felt so fantastic to touch you. Your skin is like silk. And your scales are so shiny and beautiful, like thousands of small, magnificent jewels.

Oh, Shen...
That was...
That was...
SLIP
SPLOSH

GASP

HA HA HA

Come to think of it, plenty of my favorite novels have a romantic bath scene.
Hehe, I've read quite a few like that too.

Shen...

Don't worry about it. It doesn't matter anymore.
I am so sorry for the life you had to live. You deserved so much better.
You had to live through so many terrible things, you have lost so much, how do you mean it does not matter? How can you say that?

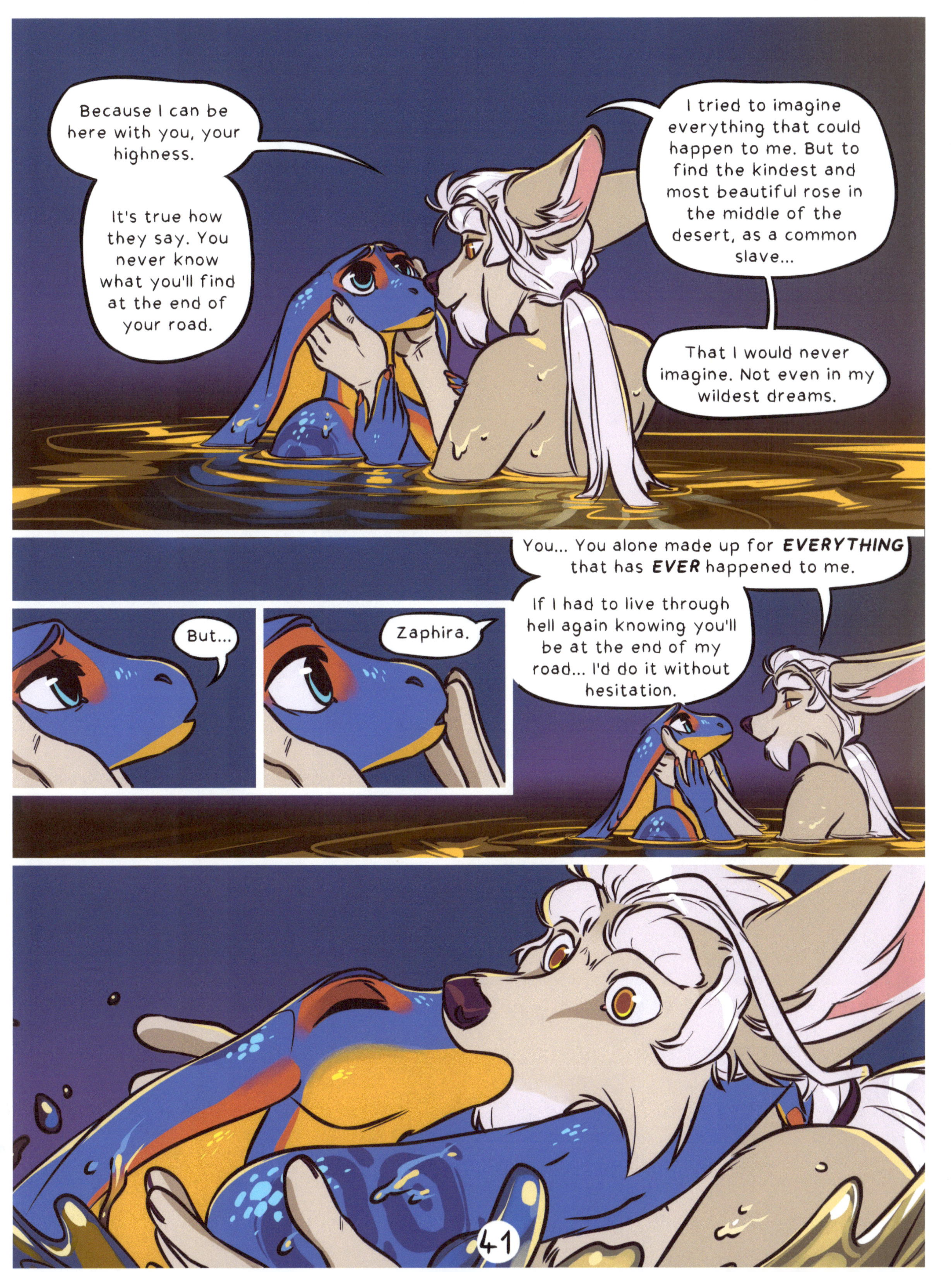

Because I can be here with you, your highness.
It's true how they say. You never know what you'll find at the end of your road.
I tried to imagine everything that could happen to me. But to find the kindest and most beautiful rose in the middle of the desert, as a common slave...
That I would never imagine. Not even in my wildest dreams.
You... You alone made up for EVERYTHING that has EVER happened to me.
But...
Zaphira.
If I had to live through hell again knowing you'll be at the end of my road... I'd do it without hesitation.

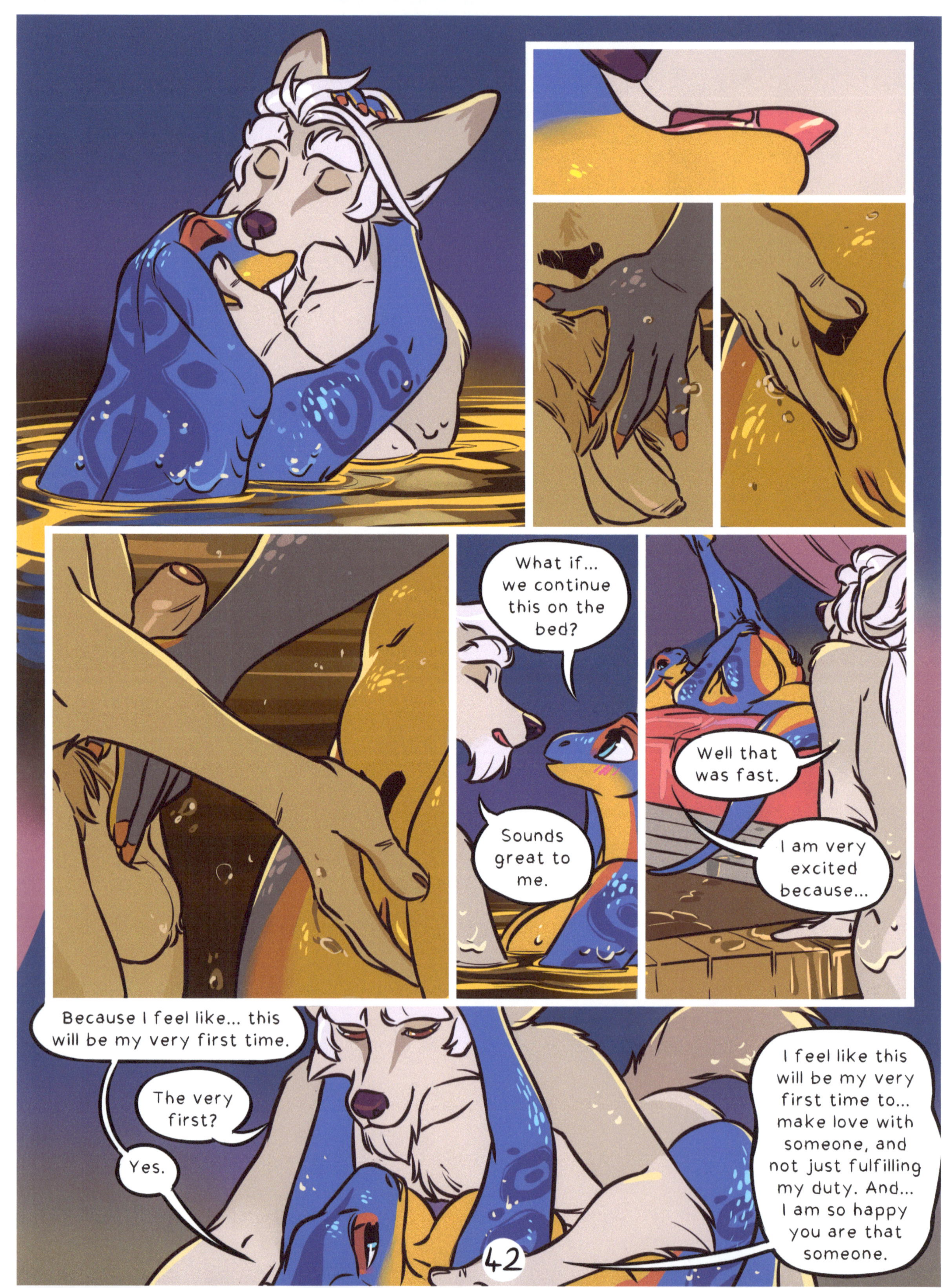

What if... we continue this on the bed?
Sounds great to me.
Well that was fast.
I am very excited because...
Because I feel like... this will be my very first time.
The very first?
Yes.
I feel like this will be my very first time to... make love with someone, and not just fulfilling my duty. And... I am so happy you are that someone.
42

For the first time, they were truly connected.
Not just their bodies, but their souls as well.
And they couldn't get enough of each other.

And...
Go on.
No, it is silly...
FLICK
Don't worry. I'm sure it won't be silly.
So...
And finally, for the first time, they embraced each other as true lovers.
Because for the first time in their life, they experienced true love...
See, I told you it won't be silly
44

That night was about endless love, and deep passion.
That night was beautiful.
That night was eternal.
But that night was even more than that.
That night was...
Please, don't be afraid to say what you feel.
That night was...
Life changing...

That's right.
After that day, both of their lives changed...
...forever.
46

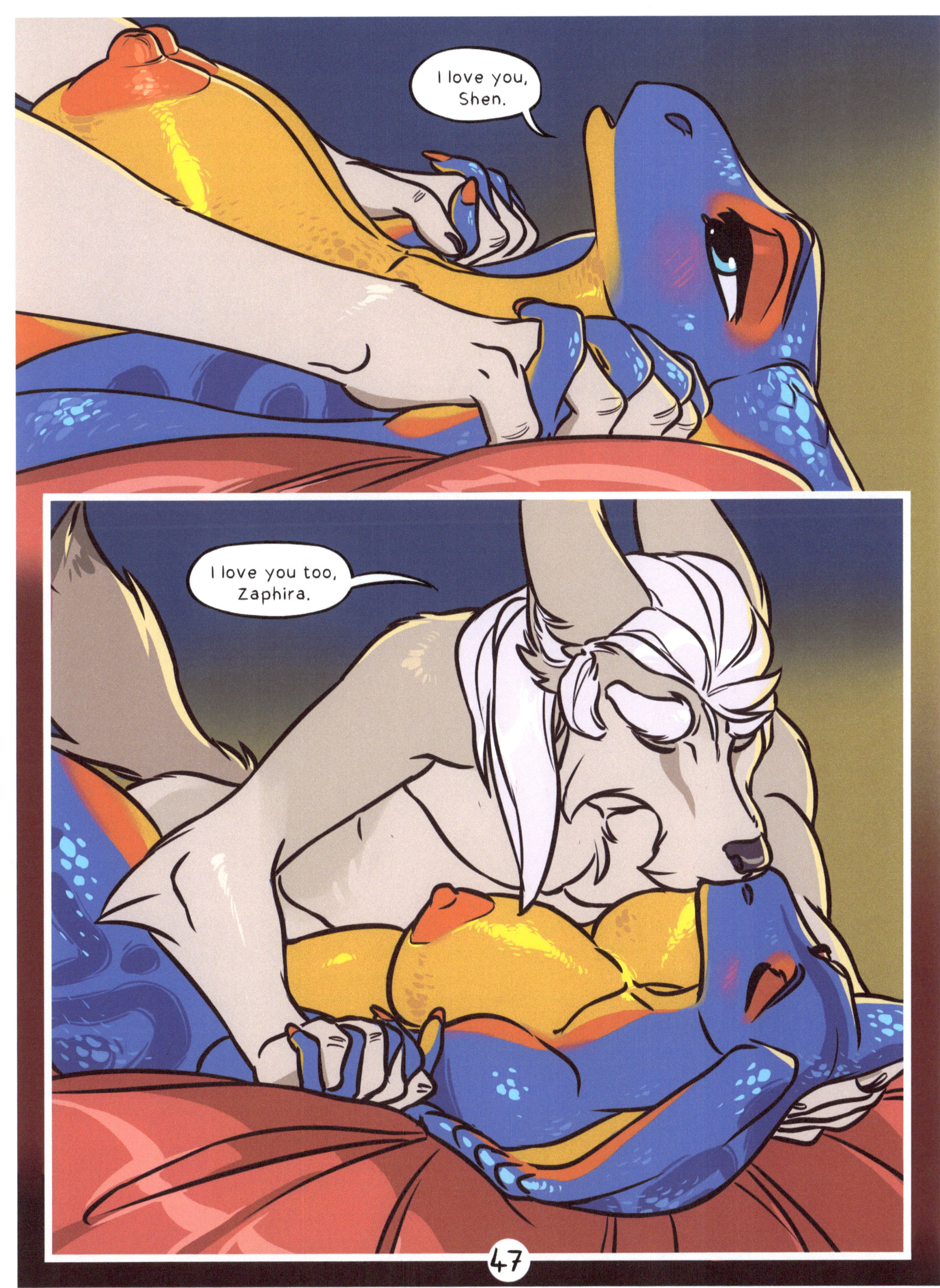

I love you, Shen.
I love you too, Zaphira.

And they kept loving each other...

...throughout the whole night.

Oh Shen...
I am exhausted...
But I do not want to stop!
I wish this night could last forever too...
49

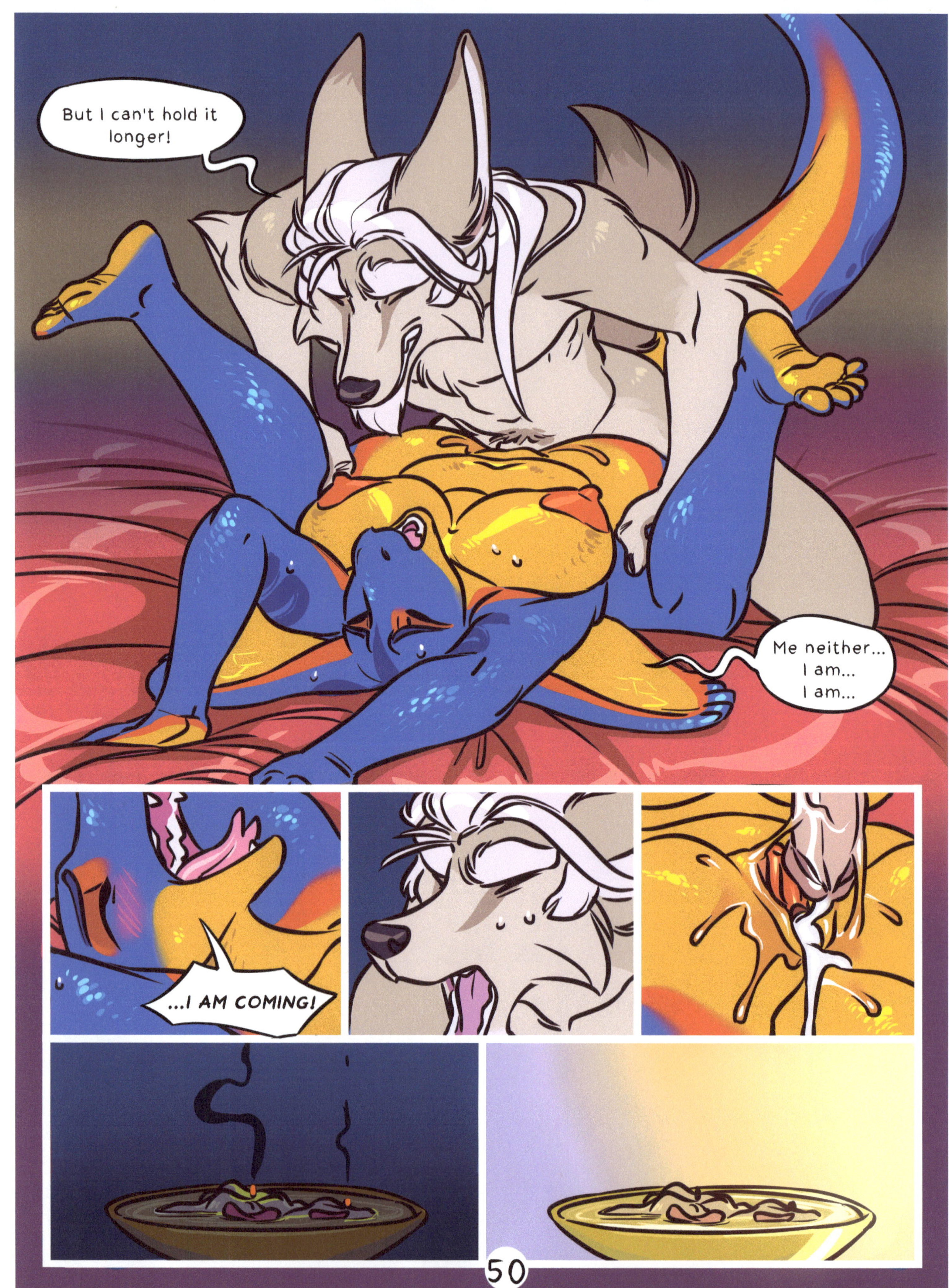

But I can't hold it longer!
Me neither... I am... I am...
...I AM COMING!

GAH!
OH NO! I FELL ASLEEP!
No, Zaphira, wait!
But the prophecy!

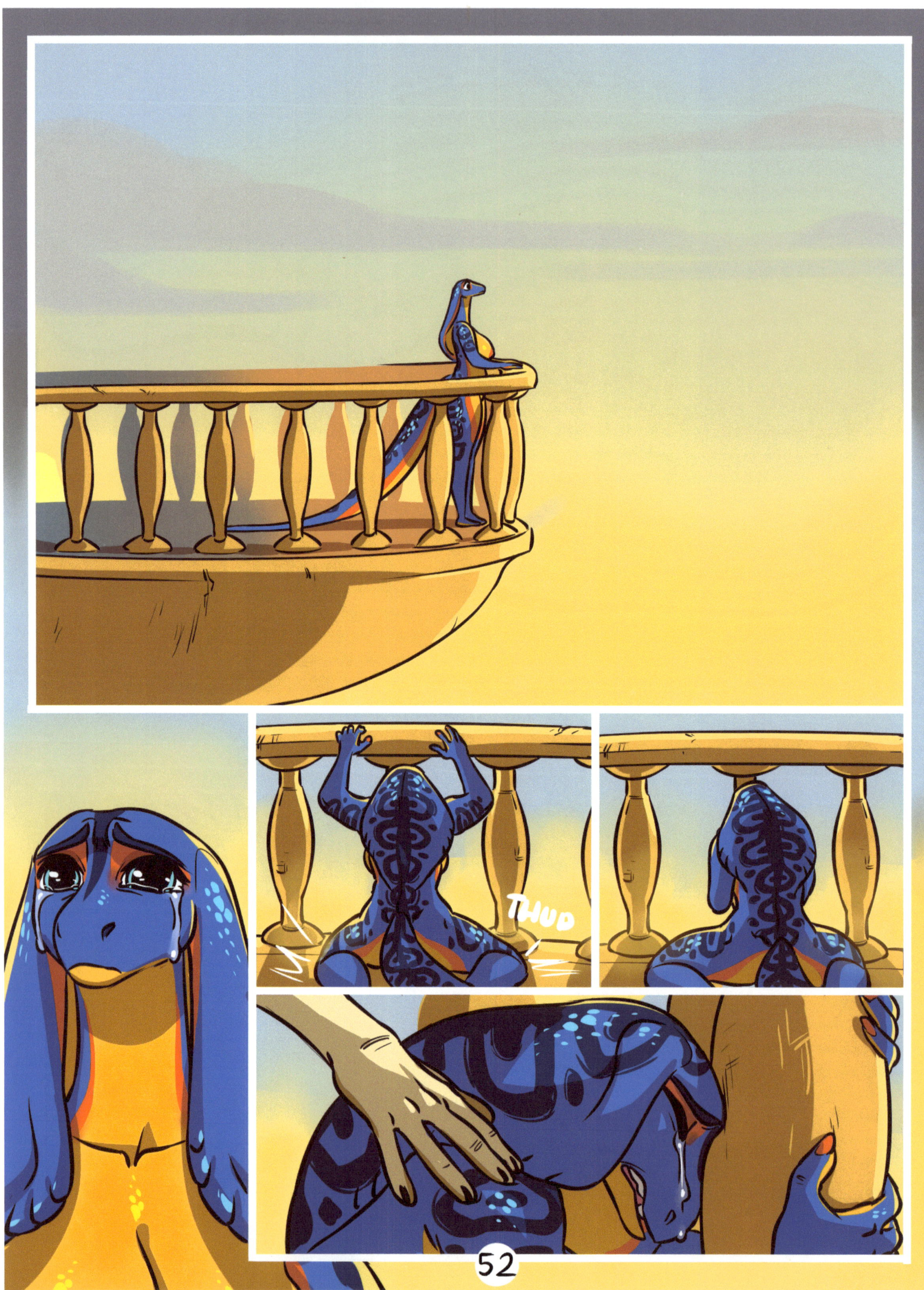
THUD

It must be all because of me...
I am not worthy for the grace of the gods... I failed everyone...
Don't say that.
My people had faith in me, and I betrayed them... They had faith in me...
You are a great and caring queen...
No! Do not call me that! I am a queen no more! The prophecy would never lie. We did find you, as it was foretold. And the prophecy was still not fulfilled...
Maybe I am not the Lock? I dedicated my whole life to help my people in the greatest of need...
I had no friends, no family, I gave everything to the prophecy... And I still failed...?
But what is this prophecy?
But I already spoke of it in details...
Did I not...?
No, you didn't. I know I'm supposed to be the Key, and you're supposed to be the Lock, but what exactly is it about? I still don't know anything about it besides its existence.
I see... All of this does not matter anymore. Nothing does... But you still deserve the explanation you should have already received from me if I would not be a failure from the very beginning...
Don't talk like that, please...
Anyway...

It was a long time ago it last rained around here. All of our water reservoirs are almost completely empty now. We could not produce crops like this, so merchants slowly started to avoid our city.

Oasis, once the most prosperous city ever in the Infinite Desert, now just a shadow of its former self.

A few more weeks and all of our storehouses will be empty... A few more months, and...
The prophecy foretold that in the time of great need, with the help of the Key and the sacred Lock, the water will return to Oasis, and the city will step into a new golden age. But there is no rain, and I can not see water either...

Is that all? That's FANTASTIC!
H-how... can you say such a thing?
How can the death of an empire be fantastic?
No, not that!

I was a well-digger before I was sold as a slave!
I could find water!
I could help!

W-why are you laughing? I'm serious...
HA HA HA
Forgive me dear Shen. But your kind naivety brings me great joy.

Please do not take it personal, but you could not even comprehend the number of people we hired from all over the globe to find water.
Hundreds and hundreds searched for any small amount of water.
Not a single one succeeded...
But what if I can find some?
What if I can help?
Shen, it is pointless...
And what if that was the prophecy all along?
What if I was destined to find water for you?
Shen...
Do not give me false hopes!
Please!
Please...
...no more false hopes...
Zaphira, I BEG OF YOU!
Just give me a chance to help!

HERE!
We have to dig here!
Are you certain? The others tried around here many times.
And they were VERY close. But not close enough.
What makes you think that?
These.
There is plenty of water under us. I can hear it!
Shen, this is insane... How could you possibly hear water from such depths?
Trust me Zaphira, this is my only talent. There is a lot of water here!
I can feel it!

Zaphira, just give me a few tools and some time. I will NOT disappoint you!

You heard him people! Give him EVERYTHING he needs!

YES YOUR HIGHNESS!

And Shen dug.

SHFF

He dug for five days...

THUNK

...and for five nights.

SHFF

SHFF

SHFF

SHFF SHFF

Without eating or drinking, he did not stop for a single moment. He dug for water like he was possessed.

Please Shen...
Please stop!
I appreciate your devotion, but it is hopeless. You will not find water here... You are only going to ruin yourself...

You know, in the past few years, there was only one thing that kept me alive.
The slavers.
Do not say that Shen...
I gave up hope a long time ago.
Do you know how many times I tried to end my own life?

Do you know how many times the slavers were forced to tie me to something, so I couldn't kill myself?
I gave up on hope a long time ago. Then you came.
You have no idea how much your struggle means to me...
But I just can not sit and watch you suffer anymore!

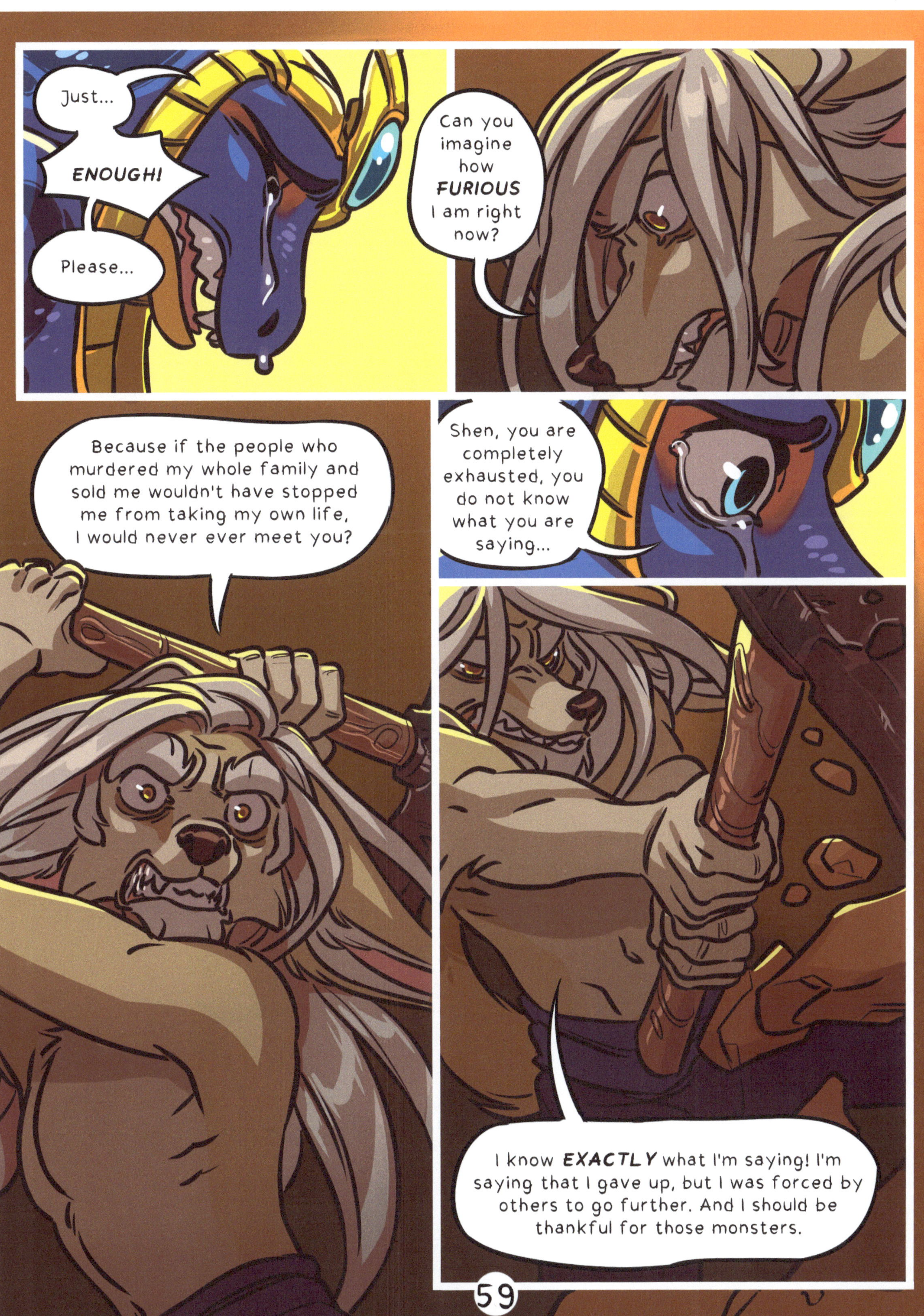

Just...

ENOUGH!

Please...

Can you imagine how FURIOUS I am right now?

Because if the people who murdered my whole family and sold me wouldn't have stopped me from taking my own life, I would never ever meet you?

Shen, you are completely exhausted, you do not know what you are saying...

I know EXACTLY what I'm saying! I'm saying that I gave up, but I was forced by others to go further. And I should be thankful for those monsters.

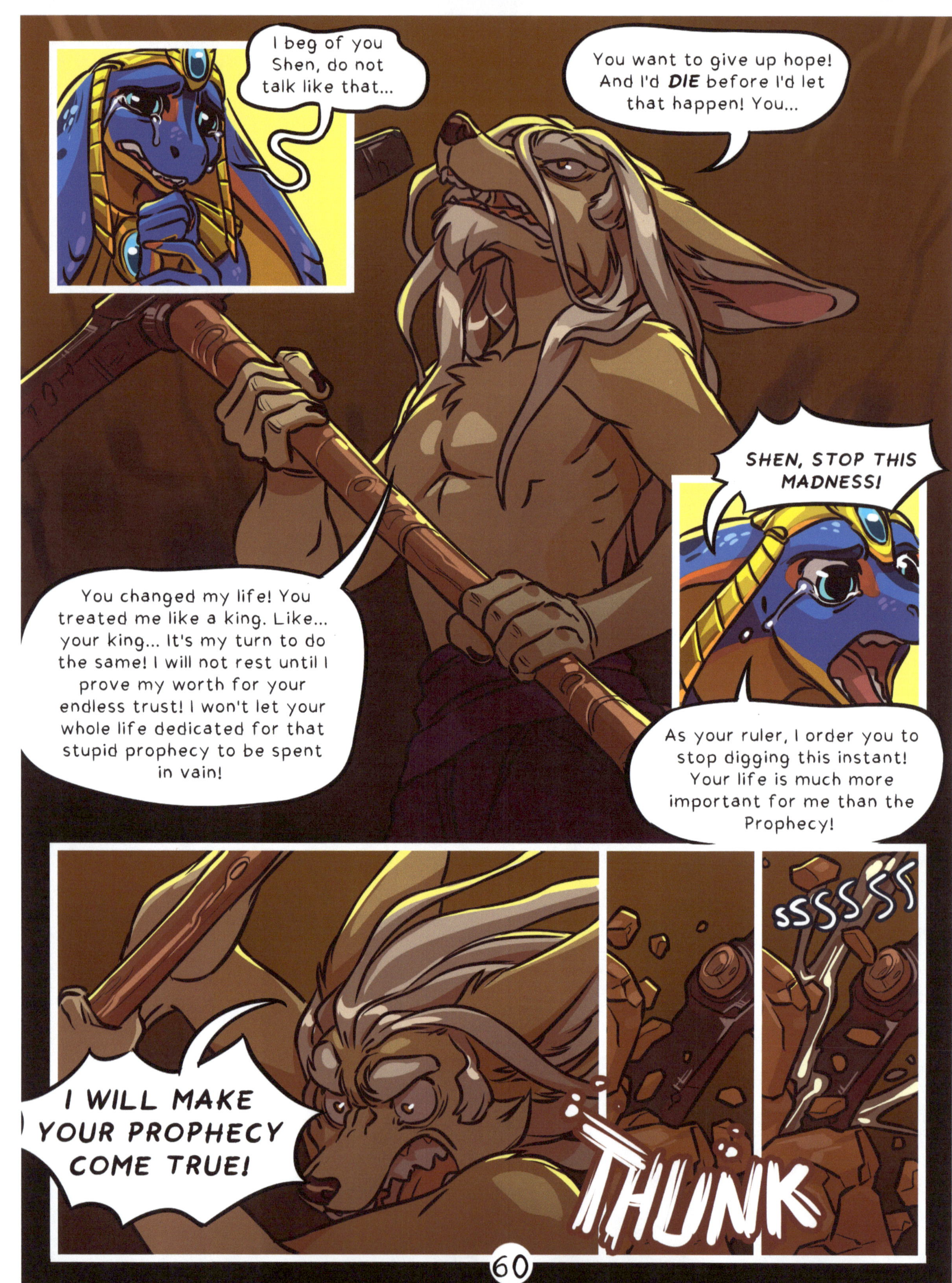

I beg of you Shen, do not talk like that...
You want to give up hope! And I'd DIE before I'd let that happen! You...
SHEN, STOP THIS MADNESS!
You changed my life! You treated me like a king. Like... your king... It's my turn to do the same! I will not rest until I prove my worth for your endless trust! I won't let your whole life dedicated for that stupid prophecy to be spent in vain!
As your ruler, I order you to stop digging this instant! Your life is much more important for me than the Prophecy!
I WILL MAKE YOUR PROPHECY COME TRUE!
SSSSSS
THUNK

FFWOOOOOSH
But this is...
This is WATER!
BY THE GODS!

I made it... I made your prophecy... come true...
OHMYGODSHEN!
Do not leave me! Not now! Not after all of this...
Yes! Got you!
Oh Shen, I was so blind! You were my prophecy all along! You saved us all!
I can not believe this! Shen, you...
I was almost the first person to drown in this desert, hehe...
After a few days, life returned to Oasis.

After a few weeks, commerce started again, and with that, the city started to bloom too.

And a few months were enough for the city to regain its former glory, to be full of cheerful noises and happiness, like it was decades ago.

So the prophecy did turn out to be true.

Because after the Key, that is Shen's heart, took it's place in the Lock, that is Zaphira's heart,...

...the two of them together turned Oasis into a prosperous city, and a prosperous empire.

Becoming truly one both in body and soul, the Key and the Lock never left each other.

And the queen of the Infinite Desert, and the slave who became a king, lived and ruled together happily ever after.

This is my favorite part!

Then you have an outstanding taste, my beautiful lady.

I just can not believe we wrote our own romantic novel!

Unbelievable isn't it?

Yes! And this is the best one ever made!

I don't know about that, but it did turn out pretty good.

Do not be so modest, my love.

And you are so good filling in the... HOLES in the story.

Oh, you really think so?

Yes! Yes I do!

Oh Shen, I want to celebrate the end of our novel!

THROB

You are a much... BIGGER writer than you think.

That's only possible because I have the BEST muse on the world.

I assume you had something in mind too?

64

And where exactly?
Oh, just follow me...
Sooo...
SMACK
Ohh, yesss...
...and you would NEVER guess what I came up with!
...I would like to continue the celebration elsewhere.
...and I show you.
POMF
Now there's my graceful queen!
You see, you taught me that in bed I should cast all my grace aside, and be as dirty as I just can!
Really? And how dirty can you be?
Oh, I can be the DIRTIEST queen of them all!

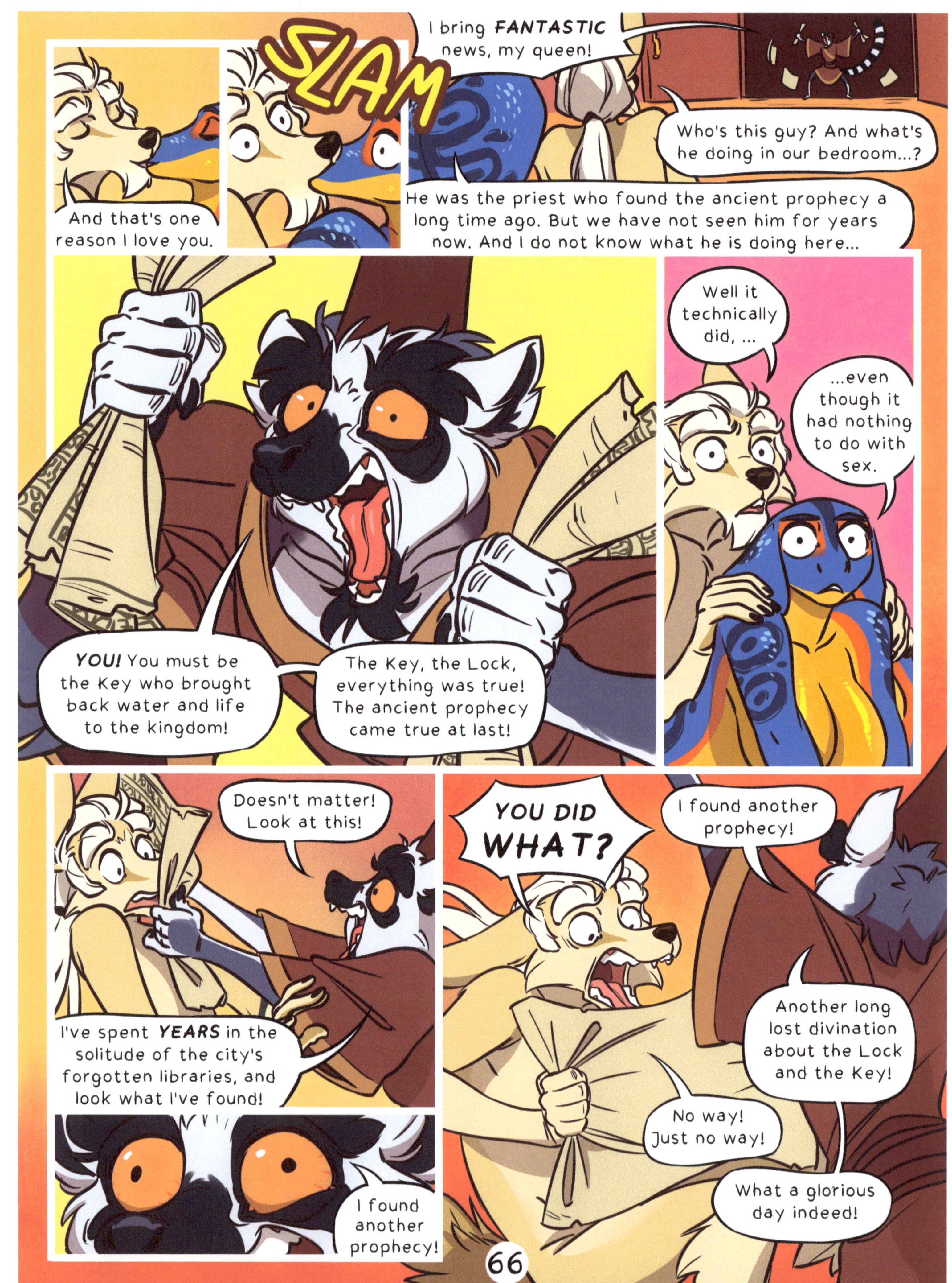
SLAM
I bring FANTASTIC news, my queen!
And that's one reason I love you.
Who's this guy? And what's he doing in our bedroom...?
He was the priest who found the ancient prophecy a long time ago. But we have not seen him for years now. And I do not know what he is doing here...
Well it technically did, ...
...even though it had nothing to do with sex.
YOU! You must be the Key who brought back water and life to the kingdom!
The Key, the Lock, everything was true! The ancient prophecy came true at last!
Doesn't matter! Look at this!
I've spent YEARS in the solitude of the city's forgotten libraries, and look what I've found!
I found another prophecy!
YOU DID WHAT?
I found another prophecy!
Another long lost divination about the Lock and the Key!
No way! Just no way!
What a glorious day indeed!

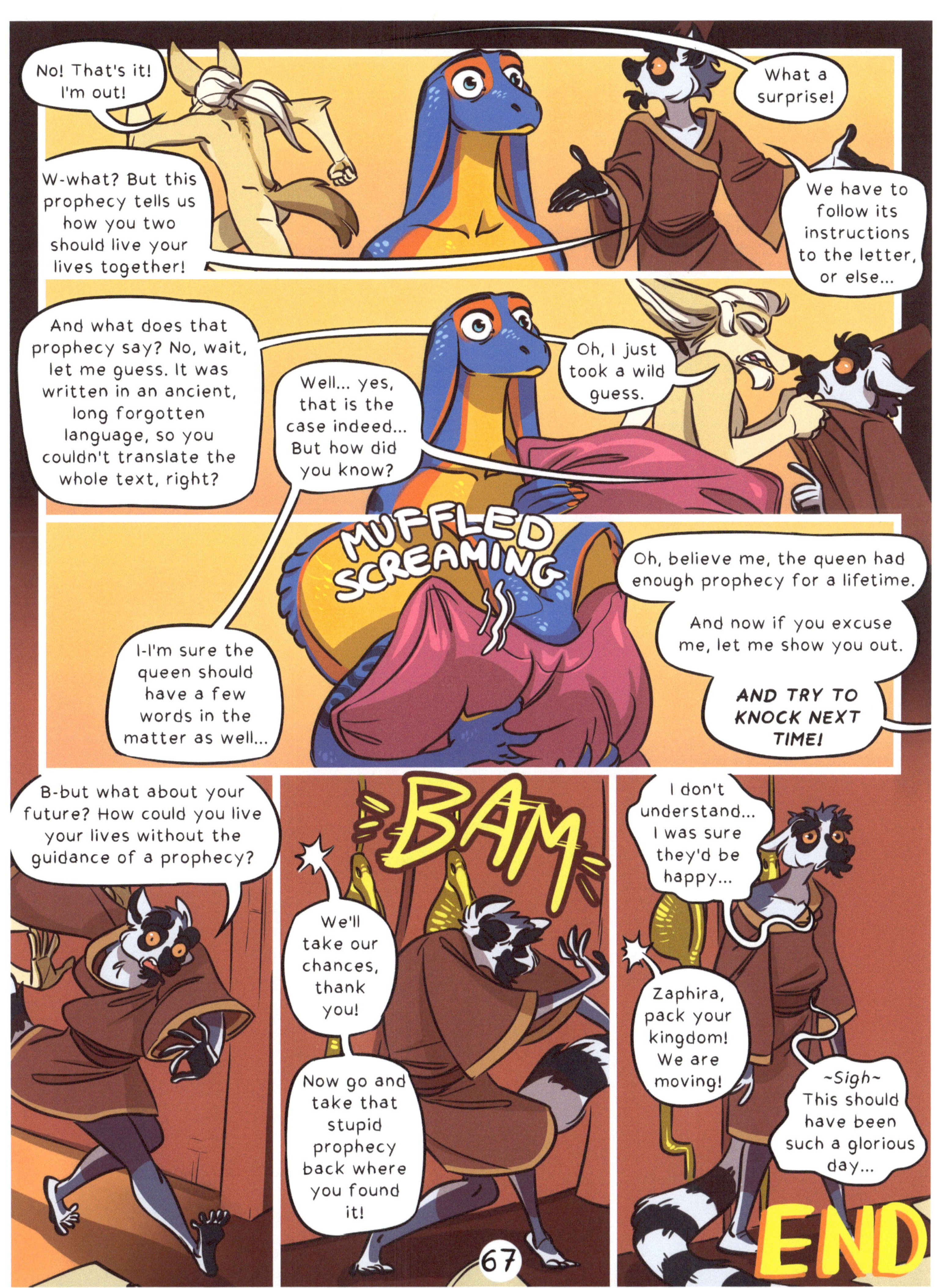

No! That's it! I'm out!
W-what? But this prophecy tells us how you two should live your lives together!
What a surprise!
We have to follow its instructions to the letter, or else...
And what does that prophecy say? No, wait, let me guess. It was written in an ancient, long forgotten language, so you couldn't translate the whole text, right?
Well... yes, that is the case indeed... But how did you know?
Oh, I just took a wild guess.
MUFFLED SCREAMING
I-I'm sure the queen should have a few words in the matter as well...
Oh, believe me, the queen had enough prophecy for a lifetime.
And now if you excuse me, let me show you out.
AND TRY TO KNOCK NEXT TIME!
B-but what about your future? How could you live your lives without the guidance of a prophecy?
BAM
We'll take our chances, thank you!
Now go and take that stupid prophecy back where you found it!
I don't understand... I was sure they'd be happy...
Zaphira, pack your kingdom! We are moving!
~Sigh~ This should have been such a glorious day...
67
END

Hi there!

I'm Zummeng, a freelance comic artist from Hungary.

I have drawn since I could hold a pencil in my hand, and I have loved coming up with stories and characters for as long as I can remember.

I always dreamed of being an artist, but I could never go to an art school. So I learned everything by looking at other artists' work, watching cartoons and reading a ton of books and comics. I love creating in all kinds of genres, be it comedy, adventure, horror or erotic. I don't know what life has in store for me, but I'm sure of one thing: I will keep making comics until the day I die, because drawing isn't just a job or a hobby for me, it's my life.

So, you can look forward to the return of Shen and Zaphira!

You can help me make comics by supporting me on Patreon:

https://www.patreon.com/zummeng

Or you can follow me or buy some merch on many other places:

https://zummeng.carrd.co/

Buy Me a Coffee
ko-fi.com/zummeng
PATREON
patreon.com/zummeng

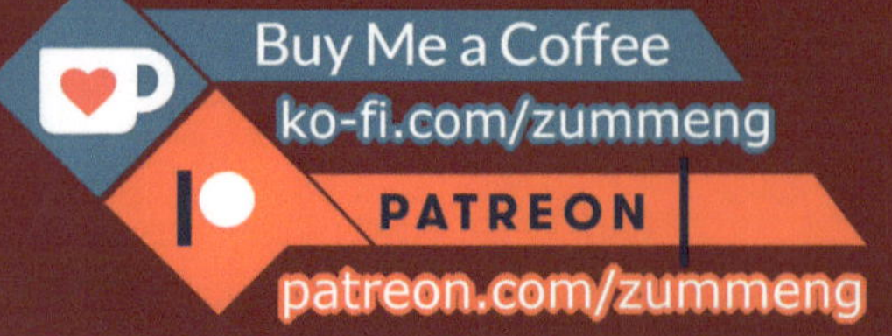

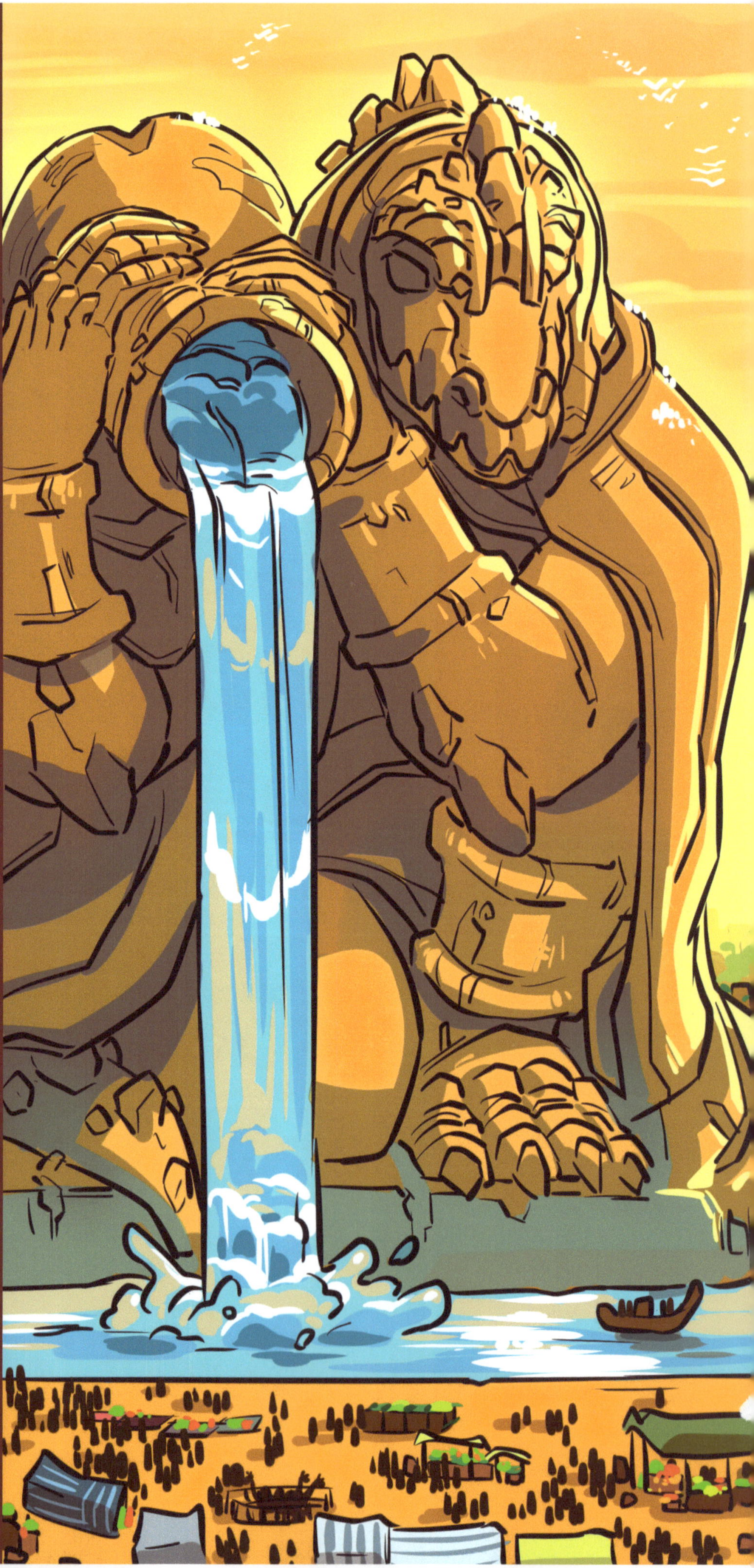